Delilah

By

Maude Stephany

Tell stories worth living!

Maude.

Edited by Yvan C. Goudard

PREFACE

Delilah, a Philistine and soon-to-be priestess of El, is under attack. The Israelites hold her city under siege and the Archangel Raphael appears in her visions, insisting that she must obey the will of the Hebrew God. Summoned to her father's scriptorium, she learns that she has been promised in marriage to her people's enemy: Samson.

Amid the Senate's political posturing and her Uncle Achaziah's plotting revenge on Samson and the Israelites for killing his sons, Delilah is wed to Samson. She returns with him to his home, but lives in isolation, except for her slave companion, Umi. Samson and Delilah have heated arguments, but when he falls ill, she nurses him to health.

In town, Delilah meets a prophet and begins to question her place in the world and the differences between her own God and the Hebrew God. Could they be the same? Meanwhile, Samson recovers but wishes to live a more private life. Before they can adjust to their new lives, Samson accidentally injures Delilah. That night, Samson comes to Delilah and offers her a knife, asking her to cut his hair as penitence for harming her. They make their peace and consummate their marriage. In darkness, Uncle Achaziah arrives and captures Samson.

Months pass, and Delilah returns to the city of her ancestors. She seeks the Oracle's advice, but the Oracle has none. In despair, she prays to El, who commands her to find her husband. She goes to the jail and finds Samson shorn and crusted in dirt. Delilah tries to reconcile with him, but he spurns her, thinking she betrayed him to her uncle. She is about to leave when Uncle Achaziah arrives to bear Samson to his trial.

Delilah faces a choice – to support her husband, to protect her people, to listen to her gods, or to follow where her dreams lead her.

CONTENTS

CHAPTER 1

"No," Delilah argued. Clouds of sweet cedar incense curled in the air around the robed figure that hovered above her. She scowled at it, wishing it would vanish. It didn't.

"The Most High demands it," Raphael said.

"I am a Daughter of El. Tell your god that I will not serve him."

"Your god and our god are one. You will obey him, whether it be your will or not." Raphael frowned, thrusting his flaming sword before him.

"Begone!" Delilah knelt before her shrine to El and focussed on the statue of her god in the light of the oil lantern. "Great El," Delilah murmured, "Heavenly Father, Just Judge, Fierce Warrior, protect your daughter from wicked spirits; send them far away."

Raphael unfolded his wings from behind his back and spread them. A sound like rocks tumbling down a mountain forced her back on her heels. Each beat of his wings pounded into her head. You will, you will, they seemed to say. He hovered higher in the room then gave a hawk-like screech as he soared over her and out the doorway. Exhausted, Delilah collapsed onto the stone floor.

Delilah knew without looking that the guard on her room had changed. Ever since the Israelites had begun their siege, her father had insisted on providing her with one, though she could not completely understand why he bothered; not when her home was one of the best protected places in the city. Any fighting in the lower city would be long contained before it would reach her in her family's home on the mountainside, her warrior uncle, Achaziah had repeatedly assured them.

Delilah's head throbbed with the memory of her vision; not unlike the reverberations of battering rams striking the city walls. The Israelites had ceased their assault on her city for the day, but the stabbing pain in her head had not vanished. No, she observed as she ran her fingers through her dark wavy hair in an effort to chase the confusing images away, her vision held her hostage. She peeked through the gauze of her hanging chair and, spying the sentry that stood by her doorway, Delilah ducked back into its coolness, away from the glare of the morning sun and the stinging bugs that came from the marshes.

Footsteps slapped on the hard rock steps. A dark skinned servant woman dressed in her traditional yellow vestments bustled into the room. Delilah watched as she looked first to the mound of cushions that served as Delilah's bed and then to the corner where the shrine to El stood. A small puddle of blood marked where Delilah had been.

"Delilah?" she called. "Where are you?"

Delilah coughed once. Umi swung around and quietly made her way to the hanging chair.

"Praise the gods," she whispered. "You are awake."

"Yes, Umi, I am awake, but my head feels like it has borne the worst of the Israelite attacks today."

"Your cycle has come a second time now," Umi pointed to the blood stain. Delilah nodded. Umi regarded Delilah carefully. "You have dreamed again."

"Yes," Delilah answered, "although it was not a dream, but a vision."

"Your mother was a powerful Seer. In her death it seems that she has given you her gift."

"You mean her curse," Delilah interrupted.

"Did you learn more?"

"Nothing I can remember." Delilah groaned. "Each time I seek the God, I wake like this." She gripped her head in emphasis.

"Speak with the Oracle, he is wise," Umi stated.

"I did, already," Delilah answered. Impatience painted her voice.

"What was his answer?"

"The usual – pray, make offerings, and isn't it time for me to consider joining the priestesses." She shrugged. "How am I supposed to tell El's Anointed One that the Hebrew God is sending his messengers to talk with me?"

Umi shook her head, swinging her tiny black braids back and forth. She pursed her thick lips. Her face looked like a dried fig.

"I do not know." Umi gasped. "I had forgotten my duty. Your father has summoned you to his library."

"Now?"

"Now."

The curtains parted, and Delilah stepped through, her purple dress flashed gold thread woven in dreamlike designs on the cloth. Her slender bronzed feet and toes touched the warm stone floor. She winced in disapproval of the sun's light in her amber eyes. Shading them, she addressed Umi.

"Fetch me water and oil for my hands; then tell my father that I am coming."

Delilah practically crept up the steps to her father's workplace. Any news that he might have to share so soon after a battle was bound to be sombre. The library was a large room, with many south-facing arched doorways to allow sunlight to enter almost all day. Its north wall was lined with scrolls which father's servant stored in their cubicles. On warm days, light and wind and warmth were allowed to pass through the arches unobstructed. Today was such a day, and Delilah walked through the arches where the usually billowing curtains hung motionless.

"Here she is," her father said, his voice sounded a bit louder and brighter than usual. Delilah smiled at him. As always, he was surrounded with scrolls upon a stone table and dressed in his white and golden robes that marked him as chief scribe. Six members of the Council, consisting of nobles and clergy, stood next to him in their robes of office. Each of them wore a face that was a mirror of her father's. So this was an official visit, Delilah thought. She nodded to the Council and smiled.

"I am obedient to the Will of El," Delilah said as she bowed to the Council and lowered her eyes to show her submission. Perhaps they have come to ask about my taking the role of the Sacred Wife of El, she thought. Her heart beat fast and her breath quickened. That was when she noticed another set of feet several paces before the council. They were covered in dark leather sandals, stained with something red. Was that blood? Delilah felt her breath catch in her throat and snapped her attention to look around.

A fierce looking stranger stood before the Council, accompanied with men who were obviously warriors fresh from battle. The warriors stood behind him, their weapons at their sides. Delilah nervously glanced at her father and back to the man in the foreground.

"You called for me Father?" Delilah asked as she shifted from one foot to the other so she could keep one eye on the one warrior, the other on her father. The warrior, she observed, had none of her father's appearance. Where her father wore his hair short-cropped, the chieftain, Delilah decided he must be the chieftain, wore his hair in long, brown wavy locks. Even his beard was long compared to her father's well groomed chin. Delilah examined the warrior and noticed that he was young; perhaps he was a boy who had become a man but a few years before. No, she decided, he wasn't as young as she was. Looking again, she saw that he bore old scars of battle on his left arm, new ones burned red against his ruddy skin. His clothes showed that he had been in battle, and he carried a blooded sword at his waist. Blood again. Ugh. Delilah took a deep breath in an effort to try to calm herself. Her efforts were useless; she gulped in his stench of sweat and blood. Delilah felt a burn as if her stomach had risen into her throat. She forced it back down. She moved toward the table where her father and the Council were gathered. Something terrible was unfolding before her; she could see it.

"Delilah, my gentle, loving daughter," her father forced a smile and rose from the table. He stepped from behind it and the gathered

Council toward where she stood. In her eyes, his reed-like frame towered over her. "Thank you for not keeping your husband-to-be waiting."

"My husband?" Delilah stepped back, uncertain if she had heard her father correctly.

"Yes, Delilah, your husband," her father said, through gritted teeth. Delilah saw him glance back at the Council. They seemed as solemn and cold as the frowning statues of El. A look that Delilah had never seen before shone from her father's eyes. If she guessed right, it looked suspiciously like fear. What was Father afraid of?

Delilah turned to the face the foreigner before her. Her dress rippled against her. "I will not marry you, you dirty…" she spat out.

"Delilah," her father interrupted. His hawk-dark eyes pierced through her. "Keep your place." Delilah started to open her mouth to protest, but her father's wrinkled fingers lay against her lips. "You have no say in this," he whispered as he shook his head in emphasis. "Matters such as these are beyond a mere woman. Still your tongue or I will send you away."

Delilah stood rooted in place. Her tongue stuck to the roof of her mouth. She felt as if she had just been slapped. Her father had never spoken like this to her before. She fought the tears that threatened to stream out her eyes. She held back the anger and bile that rose into her mouth. She bit on her bottom lip to stop quivering then drew sharp quick breaths to clear her mind and forced herself to listen.

"Please excuse my daughter's outburst, the day's events have over-stimulated her mild temperament," Father said to the Chieftain. "Now that you have seen her, are you satisfied?" he asked.

"She is as beautiful as I was told," answered the Chieftain. "I'll take her." He smiled as he turned to leave the library. "My men will make arrangements with you for the marriage."

"We will wait for your instructions," her father answered flatly.

The Chieftain began to walk out the arches as his guards and the city guards fell into line behind him.

Delilah felt the roiling emotions inside her rise at the sight of her usually strong father taking commands from some youth. The fire inside her belly erupted. "Who do you think you are, ordering my father around," she yelled at the Chieftain's back.

Her father met her outburst with uncomfortable silence.

A strong deep voice sounded from the man beside her. "I am Samson," he answered.

CHAPTER 2

Delilah felt like lightning had struck her; numb and tingly at the same time. This was Samson, the foe that her uncle Achaziah had berated every time the Israelites had attacked her city? He was supposed to be a soldier of legend, a fierce and terrible fighter. She examined him more closely. He had a warrior's physique, muscular and bronzed from the sun and wind and battle. If he wasn't my enemy, I might appreciate him more, she thought. His brown eagle eyes caught her appraising him. His lips curled into a smile.

"I will come for Delilah at sunset," Samson said to her father. "We will be wed according to your custom; then she will come with me and learn to love my family and serve my God."

Delilah's father nodded gravely, giving his assent. "Tonight then; we await your preparations."

Samson turned and strode out like the commander that he was; his men followed in formation, ensuring his safety, Delilah was certain. Several members of the Council filed out the doorway behind Samson. Only now did Delilah notice the soldiers who had stood with the Council. Senator Erez, a long time family friend, remained. He put his hand on Father's shoulder.

"Ravid," Senator Erez said, his face gaunt and wrinkled. "I am sorry the burden should fall to you and your family. You have already lost so much."

"I bear my burden to serve my God," Father answered. His voice sounded as brittle and dry as the desert.

"Ravid. Do not be harsh with me!" Senator Erez scolded lovingly, "I tried to shield Delilah from this fate, but the Council demanded it."

Ravid shrugged his shoulders and stepped away from the Senator, "I do not want your comfort now, leave me to my family while I still have one." Delilah could taste the bitterness in his tone like carob powder on her tongue. The Senator nodded. His robes swished on the stone floor as he passed through the doorway and left Delilah alone with her Father.

"Please Father," Delilah pled. She pulled on his arm and turned to face him, "you can not be serious about this union." She pouted in an effort to play on her father's sympathies. She saw the gravity in his eyes when he answered her.

"Yes, Delilah, I am," he said. Bushy white eyebrows framed his dark eyes.

"Why was I chosen then, Father?"

"He wants a powerful woman."

"I'm not important. I am just a postulant to the Servant of El. He could have chosen her. Why me?" Delilah interrupted.

"Come sit beside me child, I will tell you." He motioned to the bench behind his worktable. Delilah remembered the first time she had come here. Her father had unrolled a scroll and pointed to the squiggles on the page and shown her the magic and power of words. Here, she remembered the warmth and comfort of her father's hand as he held hers and helped her dip her quill into the pungent black ink to make her first words. Oh, this wonderful bench. Why did she feel chilled as she prepared to sit on it now?

She waited for her father to seat himself and then sat facing him, trying hard to stay still and focus on listening rather than chattering like her father forever accused her of.

"Samson wished to find a powerful virgin, Delilah." She opened her mouth to speak, but her father raised his hand to silence her words. "Of all the postulants, you are the only one who has not yet been partnered." He paused, then searched her eyes for confirmation. Delilah stared blankly back at him.

"Or have you," he asked.

"Father!" Delilah blushed. "You know I would have told you." Or more that Umi would have told you, Delilah thought. There was little that happened in her father's house that Umi didn't know.

Her father's shoulders slumped.

"Then there is no reason not to go forward with this. The Council has commanded it, and the Gods shall bless it."

"But he is an Israelite!" Delilah argued, "An unbeliever! How can the Gods bless our union?"

"We do not question the will of the Gods, Delilah. They are mysterious and powerful. Perhaps there is a lesson to be learned." He heaved a sigh. "There is more," he said, taking her hand in his. "Your cousins were killed today in the marketplace. Your Uncle Achaziah wants to attack Samson and his army right away while they are still in the city. But we cannot break our oaths of peace. The gods would certainly punish us."

Delilah suddenly understood what her destiny held. She knew how sometimes a girl from an influential family would become a wife to appease a warring tribe. Delilah bowed her head to disguise her disgust at the thought of being bartered like a cow or a goat. Her stomach gave an uneasy groan. The command that she must be a virgin, though, was unusual to her. Why would Samson place a value on such a thing? Perhaps this marriage is El's punishment, or a test, she thought. Yes, it is a test. That is all it could be.

Delilah took a quick breath, her mind, if not her heart, resolved to her course of action. She raised her amber eyes to meet her father's. Determination and strength shone from her. "I do not like it father, this Samson is…" her words lingered in the air. "But if it will buy peace for my family and our people, I will do it."

"It brings me no joy to send you to this Israelite for marriage. You know I have worked to have you accepted as a Priestess at the temple. You would have been a woman of power, and now this…" Her father took her slender golden face into his hands. He looked into her eyes as if seeing her for the last time as a child. "Thank you, Delilah. You are my daughter, and a daughter of the Gods. They will surely bless you."

Delilah wandered through her home and returned to her rooms. Her mind swam with confusing thoughts. Umi brought refreshments and food for her to take in the shade. As she lounged on her gold-trimmed cushions, Umi poured cool wine into her goblet. She nibbled on flatbread with chickpea spread as her headache slowly disappeared.

"Umi, tell me about the Israelites," Delilah said motioning for Umi to sit beside her. "You have travelled far. You know these things better than I would."

Umi sat down next to her mistress and popped a honey date into her mouth. She chewed her words and her food carefully.

"I was a child when raiders came to my village. They took me, made me a slave. On the way to Egypt, I prayed to Yemaya and she brought rain. The river flooded and the boat crashed on the shore. I wandered alone until Hebrew priests found me and brought me to their home in the desert." She paused as she took a piece of flatbread. "Their god is harsh like blowing sand. His people so fear him that they dare not say his true name. Instead, they call him El-Oh-Haim. His laws are many, and the ways to clean and dress ..." She sighed. "I prayed to Yemaya to help me, but when they found my shrines to her, they whipped and beat me; they tried to take my goddess away from me. One day, I ran to the desert. I followed the mountains and forests until I came here. Your father was a Captain; he found me hungry and almost dead. He took care of me. Now I serve your family all the while I still dream of my home."

Delilah considered Umi's words. She despaired at the thought of marrying Samson and having to take up his foreign ways. How could she follow his strange Israelite practices? How could she forsake her loving El? How could she walk away from her father and their family and not suffer great pain? Delilah rose from her purple pillows and paced her room.

Her steps led her through the gardens surrounding her home. The fragrant smell of roses mingled with the sweet dark scent of dried figs. A few unpicked fruits hung on the branches of the fig trees that lined the terrace. Songbirds flitted through the cedar hedges and stole a fruit or two. Her usual feelings of peace were broken when she came upon Uncle Achaziah pacing the terrace, grief-stricken with the loss of his sons.

"What I wouldn't give to get my hands on that Samson," he said, mumbling. "I'd kill that bloodthirsty demon with my bare hands. How could he take my sons? It's unbearable!"

"Uncle, come sit with me," Delilah said, motioning to a stone bench beneath a fig tree, "I will call Umi to fetch wine and we can drink together. It will calm your mind."

"I am undone, Delilah. I have lost my two sons to this monster. Now my niece is to be married to him."

"Yes Uncle, my marriage is tonight." Delilah sighed.

Achaziah nodded. "Tonight, I bury my sons." He bowed his head and wept. "If only they had not joined the militia. They were too young for service. But you know your cousins; they were so headstrong and so full of vigor." He searched Delilah's face for agreement and found it. "Where others ran away, they ran into battle and straight into the arms of the god of war, Reshef. He cut them down like Anat when she slew Mot when he ate Ba'al." His body trembled with anger. "Samson is lucky I have not met up with him, or I would do to him what he did to your cousins."

"And that would end the peace, wouldn't it Uncle?"

"Yes, Delilah, it would," he said, sighing in resignation. "But your cousins would be avenged, and you would not have to give yourself to this unworthy…" he began to swing his arms in exasperation.

"Uncle," Delilah said. She took his hands in hers, "Be at peace. Go prepare yourself to make offerings to Mot. You know that Mot will help them rise again, in a new life with our family once more. And although I cannot be with you, take this with you as an offering so that they will find their way to the sun again." Delilah plucked a fig from the tree and placed it in her uncle's hand.

"Thank you, Delilah," Uncle Achaziah whispered as he stared at the gift. "What a loss for our family and our people. You could have become the greatest Priestess of our time." He stopped mid-thought and smiled suddenly. "But with you as his wife, Samson could be vulnerable."

Delilah knit her brows in confusion.

"You would be able to find his flaw. Discover how to kill him," Uncle Achaziah explained. "You would know, Delilah, as his wife. Promise me you will tell us and help us destroy him."

Could I do that, Delilah asked herself. I am about to be married to my people's enemy. I do not like this at all, and I have no desire to be an Israelite's wife. If I help to destroy Samson, I protect my people from the Isaelites' attack for a time. Delilah chewed her bottom lip. But I would dishonor the gods and their command to be his wife. My family has been broken once more. She twisted her hair around her finger. How many more pieces must be lost before we can be together again? She saw Achaziah staring at her, waiting for an answer.

"Yes, Uncle, I will," Delilah answered.

"I must go," Achaziah rose. His long strides carried him through the garden, leaving Delilah alone. She sat on the stone bench watching the slaves working in the fig grove. Their black bodies shone in the heat of the sun as they worked to pick the last of the fruits from the trees. Though I am not to be their Priestess, I am still a servant of the gods, being used as these servants are made to do the gods' work. I will have to listen carefully to make certain I serve the gods well. The sun dropped lower in the sky. What will come at the sunset? Delilah wondered. What is Samson really like? How will I ever come to love him? Will he ever love me? Or will I be simply one of his many wives that a powerful man such as he must have?

Umi rushed out to her, an anxious look on her usually smiling face.

"He is not going to wait forever, Delilah." Umi took Delilah by the arm, pulling her toward her rooms. "Come, you must make ready."

"Oh, Umi! I've forgotten to do the rites and offerings to Asherah and Ba'al before a marriage. What will I do?"

"Say them in your bath," Umi smiled in a womanly way, "Samson wants his wife."

CHAPTER 3

Umi spent hours preparing Delilah for the marriage rite, bathing, anointing, dressing and painting her. She looked at her reflection in the polished bronze mirror. Delilah almost didn't recognize herself under the dark kohled eyes and red painted lips, though she admitted to herself that the effect accentuated her warm glowing complexion. She was enveloped in a cloud of scents, her body anointed with sacred oils. Golden serpent bands encircled Delilah's arms. Until today, Delilah thought, these jewels had been meant for another purpose. Umi lifted a golden net and placed it upon Delilah's dark hair. Today, she pondered, the crown of El she wore would become her bridal crown. Her ankles felt heavy with the bell anklets that Umi draped across them. Until today, they had been meant to announce her presence as Priestess of El. That was before her future had been bartered for the freedom of her city, before she had been promised in marriage to Israel's most powerful fighter.

Rather than feeling radiant, Delilah felt heavy. I'll just be a spoil of war, she reflected, another trophy to boast about. Delilah watched as Umi added one shining bangle after another. Each piece of jewelry seemed to press her into the ground. I'll just be some warrior's wife and he won't talk to me or... She felt her knees buckle as if she was going to tip to one side and then felt Umi's hand hold her upright.

"You are a strong woman." Umi smiled with confidence at her and pointed to her reflection in the pool. Delilah blinked as the sun shone off the water. She shivered at Umi's shape which was a dark shadow beside her. Delilah glittered from her golden hair net to her toes adorned in embroidered gold slippers. Wiry golden earrings hung off her ears; her gown rippled and sparkled with her smallest movement, followed by the jingling of tiny golden bells.

Delilah should have felt as light as the fine gauze linens that draped her body. Instead, she dreaded this day with every part of her being. Normally a woman was led to the marriage canopy by her mother and sisters. When her mother died of plague, Delilah's last female relative had gone to Mot. The only woman who would be with her on this day was a slave; and then, she was only allowed as witness, not as her best friend or trusted counsellor.

The Priestess' arrival was announced with the reedy drone of the zurna and the scraping, sharp drumming of the zarb. The procession arrived at Delilah's room and stopped. The Priestess stepped forward in her white robes. Her golden arm bands were wide and serpentine, symbolizing her connection to the Serpent goddess Asherah; her head was adorned with the azure blue stones of the sky god, Ba'al. Her crown held the horns of the mighty Bull of the Mountain, El the Merciful Father. The Priestess' ruby lips curved in an enigmatic smile. She rose on tip toe to whisper seven words in Delilah's ear: the same seven words that were spoken to every woman about to be married. Seven attendants came forward, their white gowns flowing as they danced and began to sing a melodic song about love, about the joy of marriage and becoming a mother.

The procession wound about Delilah, singing and dancing. The dancers cast red and pink rose petals upon the ground. The drummer and musicians took up the melody again; this time Delilah followed, releasing the scent into the air where she stepped. Umi fell into line behind the last dancer, dark and silent. The column wound through her father's house, granting her what seemed to be a last look at her paternal home. This was the home where she had been birthed, and her mother had died. This was the home that had been her sanctuary from the summer's heat and winter's cool mountain air. This was the home that had protected her in times of war. It was the same home that would deliver her to her people's mortal enemy. Where was its protection now?

The sun was halfway through its downward arc when they reached the terrace and the fig trees. All that remained on the thin branches were the dried husks that had not yet been picked. The family altar was prepared beneath the family canopy. A songbird chirped in its cage; it was a sacrifice to the gods, in hopes of a blessed union.

Father stood before the altar, Samson stood beside him beneath the canopy, symbol of their new home, waiting for Delilah to arrive.

The Priestess's parade spiraled around the altar and the guests. Delilah saw her husband for the first time without his armor or weapon. He wore a simple striped tunic tied with a leather belt and sandals. Seven times, the Priestess led them around the altar. Each time brought her closer to standing next to Samson. He had bathed, she saw, his hair and beard were dark, wavy and combed, and the strong earthy smell of sandalwood oil clung to him. A dark haired man in a plain maroon tunic stood next to Samson. The sour look on his face seemed to speak of his displeasure at the ceremony about to take place.

The procession stopped, Delilah stood to the left of Samson, and looked to Umi who was now beside her father. Umi's eyes were stone-cold, impenetrable like her father's. The silence between them was hard on Delilah; how was she to read it? Was it acceptance or grudging obedience to the Council and the need for witnesses?

The Priestess stood behind the altar and raised her arms dramatically, mimicking the form of the horns upon her head.

"Merciful El, Holy Father and Creator," she intoned. She twisted her arms in serpentine forms, "Mother Asherah, she-serpent, lion-rider." She struck a stone before her and sparks flew into the half-glow of the sun, "Blessed Ba'al, thunder clap, burning brightness and gift of life, we call you and ask that you stand witness to this union of Samson and Delilah."

The Priestess walked in a stately manner around the altar until she stood directly before the couple.

"Speak now your oaths to one another," she commanded.

Delilah looked to Samson and waited to hear what his oath would be.

"I am Samson. This is Delilah. I will give her a home and provide her with food. I will care for her as a prized calf. I will keep her safe from harm. El help me be fair and just, Asherah give me comfort. Ba'al let my seed be strong."

Delilah could not believe her ears. Samson knew the invocations of the gods. Where had he learned such a thing, she wondered. Effortlessly, she spoke the woman's response to the sacred marriage.

"I am Delilah. This is Samson. I will go with him and live in his home. I will honor his family. El show me your mercy, Asherah give me strength, and Ba'al let my tears be few."

The Priestess lifted a bowl from the altar and dipped her fingers into the clear water in it. She showered the couple before her, and pronounced a blessing. "May your joy fall like rain from Ba'al." She unwrapped a silver serpent coil from her arm and entwined it around Samson's and Delilah's hands. "May the beauty of Asherah be yours." She turned to the altar and held out the horn of a bull. "May the wisdom of El be your strength," she said as she extended it first to Samson then to Delilah who raised it to their lips to drink the holy wine contained within.

The Priestess accepted the horn from them, and passed it around to all the others gathered. Delilah watched the blank faces of her father and Umi. The dark-haired man next to them looked fearful, as if he expected lightning to rain from the heavens despite the clear sky. The man sniffed suspiciously when the horn came to him, but took a small sip. He immediately spat it out upon the ground. Disgust was written on his face as he handed the horn back to the Priestess. She met his frown with one of her own.

"Now you are husband and wife," she announced to the couple, "let us lead you to the feast!" The musicians took up their instruments. The zarb players beat a steady double heartbeat, symbolic of the two hearts that beat in a marriage. The zurna player played a lively tune that entwined the two rhythms and made them one. The marriage parade snaked around Delilah and Samson, whose arms were still entwined with the serpent coil, leaving room for them to follow to the room in which the wedding feast would take place. It slithered its way through the halls of her father's house, no longer her house, Delilah observed with melancholy. This was her father's home now. Soon her home would be with Samson. She chanced a glance at him, trying hard not to let tears fall. She felt burdened despite the constant jingling of her ankles and wrists.

Over the cacophony of jubilant music, Delilah heard the slow, steady beat of a funeral procession, its melody weaving a counterpoint to the mirthful procession she was in. The sound of the drum increased in volume the closer they came to the house, and toward the west-facing rooms. The wedding party rounded a corner and came face to face with the funeral march.

The processions met and intertwined, each led by their priesthood. The Priestess of Ba'al wove them through the funerary procession. For his part, the Priest of Mot, god of death and rebirth, led the way. Followed by two pallets borne by slaves, he circled before the newly married couple. Seeing her young cousin's wounds through the gauze, Delilah could feel nothing but hatred toward their attacker, her husband.

Samson avoided the gaze of the priest and refused to acknowledge the pallets before him. Instead he looked to her, and smiled. How can he smile at me, Delilah thought with anger, doesn't he know that these are my cousins? Delilah's eyes met her uncle's sombre eyes, trying to apologize. She thought she saw a look of hatred cross his face when he glanced at Samson but his face softened as he took in the sight of his niece one last time. He gave Delilah a half-smile and followed the Priest and the pallets away toward the family tomb. The drums beat heavily, and the processions moved along, snaking to their different destinations.

Delilah knew that her cousins would be resting in her family's home for the ancestors before the night was done. The attendants would lay their bodies in clay jars, like the ones that they had broken that day in the marketplace, their bodies covered in oil. The Priest of Mot would say final prayers with her Uncle Achaziah and leave an offering to ensure that the ancestors were content. She wished that she could have given them one last offering before they began their journey in the underworld. And yet, she considered, she had been able to take part in their funeral procession, with a gift that had been from the gods.

The shrill trill of the pipes brought Delilah back to the moment. The procession had come to a halt at the room that had been prepared for the feast. It was bathed in the warm light of the setting sun. The priestess led the newly married couple to a lounging chair covered in cushions, close to an ancestral shrine. A glowing oil pot illuminated jewels and an offering bowl upon it. A nearby table had been laid with all manner of foods. Delilah's father took up the pallet to the other side of the ancestral shrine. Umi looked uncomfortably at Delilah and then at Father before taking her place at a pallet.

"This is a horrible omen," the man in the maroon tunic said to Samson. "Life and Death have met at your marriage. This is unlawful. This is…"

"Zeev," Samson called teasingly to him, "try to enjoy yourself. This is a celebration, you know." Zeev chose a pallet to Samson's right and turned to face the door. Suspicion lined his face.

The Priestess handed Delilah a tiny cup, and addressed her solemnly.

"Remember your ancestors, Delilah. Tonight will be your last among your family." She looked sourly at Samson. "Soon you shall have to honor those of your husband."

Delilah lifted the cup to her lips, tasted it and coughed. The wine had not been diluted, as it usually was, because of the joyous occasion. She poured the remnants of the cup into the offering bowl. The thick red liquid sank to the bottom of the bowl and down through the tube that would empty into the ancestor's bowl in the crypt. Her wish to give her cousins parting gifts had been satisfied.

"The ancestors thank you, Delilah. Be well, Daughter of El." The Priestess stepped back from the couple and quickly left the room. The musicians remained and, sitting in the corner of the room, took up a gentle tune. The tabla beat softly as a musician began to pluck the lyre melodically. Slaves came and laid delicate morsels before the still bound couple. Samson and Delilah took turns feeding each other, sampling one piece at a time. It seemed as if Samson was enjoying himself; he flirted with Delilah. He sucked at her fingers and nuzzled her ears. Delilah blushed, and not entirely from the effects of the wine that the attendants continued to pour into the newlywed's goblet. Lying next to Samson, she could feel his fighter's body through the striped tunic. He was all muscle and sinew, strong and firm.

Delilah observed how Zeev and Umi seemed equal partners in discomfort. Umi who had served Delilah and her father as long as she could remember, squirmed as attendants presented her with one exquisite food after another. Delilah listened as Zeev asked the same question as each food was presented to him.

"Is this food lawful?" he asked. From the look on his face, he was unsatisfied with every answer. Zeev stared in disapproval as Samson nibbled on goat ribs drenched in curdled milk, minced pork and couscous stuffed in grape leaves, and all manner of other special fare that was reserved for the marriage feast. Zeev, Delilah observed, ate nothing but the flatbread. Her father, with whom she had usually spent hours discussing the inner workings of temple politics and Philistine history and legend, spoke in short sentences or half-thoughts. More than once Delilah observed that he had been staring at her with the hollow dark eyes of a man who had lost everything he loved.

The sun's light dimmed. Slaves rushed to light oil pots, which cast glowing orbs of light into the darkness of the room. The musicians, taking a cue, changed the intensity of the music. The rhythm switched to a hurried beat and was accompanied with the sultry drone of several zurnas. Suddenly Samson twisted the silver serpent coil off his wrist and rose to his feet. Delilah felt a gasp escape her mouth and watched as Umi and Father also stared aghast. What curse would the Serpent Mother bring upon them for Samson's unbinding of their arms? Did he not know that he could only be unbound once the marriage had been consummated? Zeev stood also, and began to dance with Samson, as was their custom. Samson stomped his feet rhythmically and Zeev answered with the same pounding pulse. It was a warrior's dance; a mock fight and a joyous victory. They are beautiful and terrible to watch, Delilah thought.

The men made to return to their pallets and called for refreshment. As attendants bustled to bring them cool mint water, the drummers beat out a rhythm that made Delilah's blood burn. It was the cue that the dancers had been waiting for. They exploded into the room, their bodies a jangle of sound and colour. Samson, already intoxicated, became caught up in the frenzy of lithe dancing women. He turned to them and attempted to dance. Zeev knit his brows into a frown and threw himself down on the opulent cushions.

"Men do not dance with women," he muttered loud enough for Delilah to hear. Samson's manly military movements seemed jerky compared to the dancers' flowing reed-like movements. He spun alongside the willowy women, and landed on top of one. She giggled and feigned an injury that required his immediate attention. Samson eyed her bronze flesh as she raised her veil seductively and swiftly turned away. Samson went to chase her, but Zeev's hand had taken hold of his arm.

"Come sit down," Zeev commanded. Samson narrowed his eyes.

"I don't want to sit down," he insisted, "I want to," he paused and stared at Delilah. She felt her body grow warm under his eyes. "I want to go to my room." So saying, he swung and took Delilah by the wrist and dragged her out of the hall. He strode down one darkened path and then turned down another. Suddenly he stopped;

Delilah bumped into him and felt the firmness of his body against the softness of hers.

"Where is it?" he asked gruffly.

"Where is what?"

"The marriage chamber," he explained, "your father said we were to have it for tonight."

"Up there," she answered as she pointed to an upper level of the house, "but it is hard to find. I had better lead," she offered. The sun gave up its last strands of light to the couple as they climbed to the upper levels. Samson's temper slowly cooled, but as it did, so also his ability to reason. The power of the Gods was upon him, Delilah noticed, and upon herself as well. She felt light-headed and barely able to stand. Gods help me get him to our room safely; I cannot carry him if he should stumble. He began to stagger as stupor overtook him and Delilah leaned into him to navigate in her own inebriation. His weight was oppressive. How was she going to make it all the way to the top of the stairs? If only I had learned the magic of herbs and medicines, she thought, I would be free of this burden. If only I had the knowledge, I could kill him now.

Zeev stepped suddenly from the shadows. Delilah jumped reflexively. Had he been watching them all this time, she wondered. Just as Samson was about to fall from her shoulder, Zeev reached her side and took Samson's weight upon his own. In uneasy silence, he bore Samson up to the marriage chamber and dropped him into a mound of cushions. He turned and left the room, his shadow a ghost at their chamber door.

Upon Zeev's departure, Delilah turned and caught her breath. She saw the chamber for the first time. Attendants had placed oil pots strategically throughout the room. Its walls were painted with friezes of men and women cavorting in sexual acts. Delilah's body colored in excitement and innocence. So this was what she was supposed to look forward to as a wife, she reflected. Still tipsy from the wine, conscious of Zeev's presence at the door, she lay next to Samson, uncertain as to how to perform the task of consummating their marriage, only to find that Samson was fast asleep. Half disappointed and half thankful, she raised a prayer.

"Passionate Asherah, I thank you. With your blessing, I will remember my marriage night and the joyful blessing of your sacred union." She inhaled the earthy scent of sandalwood that clung to him. The scent of the sky god. As she lay next to Samson feeling his warmth and strength beside her, she wondered what would come next.

CHAPTER 4

Delilah had never imagined how dirt could hurt a body. She felt grimy from head to toe. Her fingernails were blackened, each crease in her flesh was caked with soil, and it hurt to sit and stand and lie and walk. Since the night that she had married Samson, she had lived in this tent-city outside of the village of Samson's kin. She missed her home on the ridge overlooking the orchards and the scent of the fig blossoms. She missed her comfortable bed and the sun-warmed floors in the morning. Most of all, she missed her heated bath and the sweet fragrant oils to adorn her body with.

Her tent was her home now, and held everything that she needed. A makeshift bed, a folding table, a chair and a container were her sole possessions, save for the clothes she kept in a trunk. Umi was also hers, a parting gift from her father. Thankfully most of her possessions were voiceless. Umi never ceased complaining. She hated living among the Israelites and spoke constantly of her desire to return to her home in the jungle of the large continent to the West.

Samson was little more than a presence that came and left, fleeting as springtime on high mountains. He had thus far avoided the consummation of their marriage, stating that he did not think it wise to flaunt their marriage among the men who were away from their wives and lovers. Delilah didn't mind, the thought of having to be intimate with the man who had severed her from her family, her people and her way of life repulsed her.

Delilah felt like a hostage rather than a bride. She never left the tent without an escort; she saw no one other than the faithful few that Samson had appointed as her guards. Samson said it was to protect her from thieves. The real danger was Samson's people.

She felt their eyes upon her every time she left the tent. She heard them as they passed, speaking about the infidel beauty and killing her before she could twist Samson's mind. That morning, Delilah had overheard the carpenters who waited to sit in council with Samson. While their language was strange to her, it was not so different that she couldn't understand.

"A pack of wild dogs has taken seven lambs that had been given to the priests for sacrifice," one man whispered, "It's a sign from the Most High!"

"Have you seen the home that he is building for her?" one asked.

"Yes, I was helping to bring the stone," answered the quarryman. "It is just like the accursed Philistines. He is even having a bath put in."

Zeev's sharp voice cut through their discussion. "Samson will see you now." Delilah heard nothing but mumbling until Samson's deep voice bellowed out "You accepted me as your judge many years ago, now build this home for me and my bride! You have until the new moon." The men shuffled out, muttering among themselves.

"It's as I feared," one whispered, "he has become more Philistine with each passing day. He no longer dresses like us, and now he makes himself a great home at the top of the mountain. We live in simple homes. He should be happy to live among us. I shall speak with the priests."

Delilah's impatience grew. She paced back and forth, unable to sit, unable to weave. The air felt oppressively warm and still. As a priestess of El, she had been at the centre of activity and importance at home. Here, she felt disconnected. Delilah poked her head out the tent flap. Zeev was standing watch again.

"Zeev, I wish to go to the marketplace." She met his frown with resolve.

"You will need a headdress, and one for your slave."

Delilah found two scarves in her trunk. Umi tied one on her braided black hair, and then tied the other over her mistress' dark locks.

Zeev led her down the hill and to the market place. She felt the eyes of the local town folk burning into her skin. Delilah saw sheep and calves and horses mingling among those gathered at market. She made a mental note to herself to ask where they kept pigs or boars. Dried fruits and fresh fruits stood on separate benches, unlike markets at home where fresh and dried foods were laid together. There were no grapes or raisins, no wine of any kind. Fresh mustard greens, and the dried seeds were hoarded like gold in a woven reed jar. Its pungent aroma lingered in the still air.

Delilah stopped and went to reach out to touch an apricot when a stick sharply rapped her on her knuckles. Surprised, she cried out. A woman glared at her and made strange hand gestures and moved her lips rapidly as she touched something shiny on her cart.

Umi looked at Delilah with concern. Zeev shook his head in disapproval.

"Touch nothing," he said. "You will despoil their food." Delilah wandered through the market. She kept her hands tightly to her sides, afraid to risk being humiliated again.

I feel as if I am moving through water, Delilah thought. Water! "Zeev," she asked, "is there a river nearby?"

"Yes," he answered. "You were not planning to bathe there, I hope." He turned toward the valley to a place where the river lay below the village. Delilah whipped off her kerchief, and soaked it in the water and did the same for Umi.

"You must always wear your kerchief, Delilah," Zeev said. "It is shameful for a woman to walk about without a head covering. Come, the evening meal will be soon and you must return to your tent." The coolness of the dampened scarf soothed the heat in her head. Delilah and Umi followed Zeev back toward the encampment.

Delilah heard shouts coming from a group of white tents at the edge of the village. Samson was yelling while a man in white clothes shook his head and pointed to the white sheep beside him. Zeev implored her to hurry as he rushed to stand before Samson. The priest was wagging his head, flapping his arms and shouting. Curses sound the same in any language, Delilah observed. She was certain that she heard him say something about a pestilence, losing your home, your wife lying with another, and your sacrifice turning black. Zeev took the rope from Samson's hand and lead him and the lamb away. Delilah kept her distance. She had already heard Samson's rage in the tent city. She had no desire to be closer to him than she had to be.

The crescent moon appeared in the night sky; in the morning Delilah and Samson ate their meal together.

"Our home is completed," Samson said as he chewed on a piece of lamb.

Delilah's thin smile hid her emotions. Her stomach felt as if she had swallowed a rock. All this time in camp, she had been certain that Samson would go back on the promises he made before her gods.

That he would not give her a home, give her adequate food or treat her as his wife. It had been her secret hope that Samson would fail, or mistreat her and she would have a reason to go back to her people. Her hopes were ground like mustard seed in a mortar. Despite their coarse home in the tents, he had honoured their oaths. He had made certain that she had everything she needed for Umi to prepare her food, adequate clothing, and that her needs were being met. Thus far, she found no fault with her husband, except for one. Perhaps that might change now that they had a home of their own, she thought. Perhaps he may take me to bed. Delilah peeked through her eyelashes at him. He was still as handsome as she remembered. She followed the outline of his body with her eyes; her thoughts made her blush. She smiled. Samson must have taken her smile for a sign of acceptance; he took her hand in his and helped her to her feet.

"Let us go see our home for ourselves, shall we?" Delilah thought she saw apprehension behind his eyes.

"Yes, let us see," Delilah nodded as she looked at his strong hand enveloped around hers. Where it touched, she felt tingling as if she had brushed nettle. She expected him to let their hands drop before they left the tent, but Samson held fast.

Since that fateful first visit, Delilah had won the grudging acceptance of the merchants in the marketplace. With Zeev and Umi to help her, she was able to conduct business. Even the villagers had ceased their hostile stares at her passing. Today, however, she felt everyone's eyes upon her; her hand in Samson's. She thought she saw anger behind their looks. She looked at him for reassurance; he smiled at her.

Delilah grew anxious, her breath came in gulps. Was Samson oblivious to the hostility that his people bore her? Or is he defiant of them? Delilah thought about that a moment, her heart pounding. What does he have to prove to them, she wondered? She noticed, then, where their path was taking them. Samson was leading her through the village and past the tent-city temple. Realization dawned on her suddenly. He is showing his tribe that he means to take me as his wife, she thought. The unease in her belly flip flopped.

They proceeded, with Umi and Zeev following, past the primitive Israelite homes of grass, wood, earth or thatch, and to the meadow that lead to the base of the mountain. With each step she took up the wide trail, she tried to prepare herself for her new life. The tangy scent of cedar filled her lungs. With each breath, she took in the purifying aroma that surrounded her. It was as if the gods themselves had prepared this place for her, this time for her to make her new beginning. Even the scrub sage lent its clarity and calmness to her mind.

Soon, they arrived at the crest of the mountain and the home that had been built. Delilah laughed uneasily at the irony of her new house.

"You are pleased, then" Samson asked, mistaking her laughter for happiness. Delilah felt her mouth dry at the thought of speaking. The home was built in the style of her people, entirely of rock and cedar.

It glistened in the morning sunlight. It was as if her father's home had been built on this mountaintop. A wave of homesickness washed over her.

"Speechless," Samson nodded. "Then it is just as I wanted for you."

Delilah managed to mumble a thank you and force a smile for her husband.

"Zeev tells me that you need instruction in our ways." Samson said. "I asked the Rabbi and his wife to come; they will begin instruction in the morning." He wrinkled his brow in thought and turned to Umi. "Can you cook?" he asked.

She nodded.

"Good," Samson said to her. "Prepare something for us to eat tonight." He paused and addressed Delilah. "I have a meeting with the council. I will see you at the evening meal." He spoke quickly with Zeev and hurried away. Delilah and Umi wandered through the house and found the balconies. Delilah stood a long time, looking out over the Valley of Sorek. The green valley lay like a ribbon to the shining city of her home. She could just make out the pillars of her father's home in the distance. She squinted her eyes at the brightness of the sun, tears trickled down her cheek. She didn't realize that Umi had come and gone until she felt her hand on her shoulder.

"I have found the baths, Delilah," she said. "Water is being poured for you."

A bath! The thought of finally ridding herself of the grime from her time in camp brought a smile to her lips.

"Umi, do you remember how to cook for these people?" Delilah asked.

"A little," Umi replied.

"Show me the bath, then. We will prepare the meal after."

CHAPTER 5

Delilah anointed herself with the sacred oil. She touched it to her forehead, upon her throat and between her breasts. She rose and bowed seven times, giving homage to the image that stood in the corner of her room. It felt good to be able to perform the rites again, to bathe in the glow of the lantern's light, to be immersed in the presence of her god. The image of El seemed to smile in acceptance of her obedience to him. She kneeled, then, and pointed her toes as she sat back on her heels. She stared at the idol, eager to find the vision of El. Her body tingled where the oil had touched. Each time she began to slip into trance, her vision blurred. All she saw was light and nothingness.

Great father, she asked, help me be a dutiful daughter. Help me know my husband and do what is right. She waited patiently, stilling her anxiety and heard a whisper in the stillness, "You are my daughter, hear and obey your god…"

Delilah's head lolled to one side. Her eyes rolled back into her head. Her body thrummed a mystic rhythm; she was immersed in trance.

There was the sudden sound of something breaking. Something shattered. She inhaled grit and dust. Chunks of clay hit her body, followed by a powder. Delilah was yanked out of her trance and forced her eyes open. Her head ached immediately with the sensation of spinning and jerking all at once. Samson stood before her, rage etched into his face. He held El's head in his clenched hand before her.

"What is this?" he asked. He trembled in anger. Delilah forced herself to look at him. Her head felt pinched and tight.

"It is El…"

"El? What is El doing in my house?" Samson stormed.

"He is my god," Delilah answered. "My god, El the Just."

"There will be no other gods here," Samson bellowed.

"We were married by the Priestess of Asherah, do you not honor my gods?"

"No!" Samson interrupted. He threw the head to the ground. It exploded, sending a fine dust all over them both. "No!" Samson swung his arm, knocking over decorative pots on the ledge. They fell and broke into shards. He kicked at them, mashing them into dust.

He started to hurl them. Shouts of "No" punctuated the sound of breaking pottery.

Delilah backed away. She sought safety behind a wall and listened as she heard Samson break one vase after another. A fine dust floated in the air.

Footsteps sounded outside the room as Umi arrived. Delilah motioned for her to stay out of the room and out of sight. Delilah cowered behind a wall which offered some protection from Samson's rage. Her heart raced, she sprinted for the corridor. Breathless, she let Umi lead her through the passages, past the kitchens, through parts of her home she had never seen. Without knowing how, she found herself in the servant's quarters, seated on the straw mat that was Umi's bed.

"Let me see you, Delilah," Umi insisted. She hovered over her like a bee over a fig blossom.

"I am fine, unhurt. See?"

"But what about next time, Delilah? What then?"

"If only I could speak with the Oracle, he would tell me what to do."

"You do not need an Oracle, Delilah, you need a plan. We need to get you out of here."

"No, Umi, if I do not stay, the Israelites will attack my home again."

"Who cares about men and their wars? Leave them to themselves; they will all kill each other. Let us run away."

"Run away? You are crazy. Where would we go?"

"To my home in the dark forests. To warmth and plenty and comfort and family."

"Family for you, Umi. Not for me. If I leave, I dishonor my family and bring danger to my people. No. I will stay. Besides, I don't think he's as bad as you think. Perhaps this is as the priestess told me – that men are like El – both gentle and wild and that the power of Asherah will gentle him."

"You are young and foolish."

"I am a daughter of El, and I will obey him and my father," Delilah asserted. Umi gave Delilah a tightlipped look.

"Then you had best get some sleep 'Daughter of El', morning will come soon."

Delilah rubbed her legs. They were cramped and sore from sleeping upon the earthen floor. Her head hurt at the thought of Samson. Perhaps she could return to her room and not have to face him. With Umi's help, she returned to her room, where her hope died. Samson was stretched out on her bed. A small brigade of servants worked to clean the mess around him. He rubbed his eyes and took a flagon of water and poured it into his mouth.

"Where were you last night?" Delilah asked.

"I was ..." Samson started.

"I was entertaining your guests," Delilah snapped.

"My guests?" Samson began, realization dawning on his face. "After the council meeting, I needed to…" He stopped. "I forgot about the priest and his wife. Did it go well?"

"No, Samson," Delilah said. Her head buzzed angrily. She frowned in frustration. "You could have told me that eating an animal in its mother's milk was forbidden."

"Tell me that you did not serve them that?!" Samson exclaimed.

"I did," Delilah said. "How am I to learn your ways if you won't take the time to teach me?"

"What am I supposed to teach you?"

"I suppose I need to learn how to cook first, if you want to eat according to your laws."

"Men do not cook. My mother did all that."

"Well, you could ask your mother to help me."

"I cannot" Samson admitted, "now that we are married, she says that I am dead to her."

Delilah couldn't imagine what he spoke of. She shook her head to show her ignorance.

"She will not speak to me; she said that you are dangerous."

"I am dangerous?" Delilah said incredulously. "You are the one who killed my cousins. You are the one who took me away from my family, my people and put me in this miserable village with nothing but sheep and goats for company."

"Oh enough," Samson shouted. He clamped his hands to his ears and bellowed, "I am leaving."

"But you have been home but a few hours."

"This is not my home, it's yours."

"This is not a home Samson, it is my prison," Delilah asserted, "and you are my jailer."

CHAPTER 6

"Your jailer? I think you are confused." Samson growled.

"No, Samson, I see you clearly now," Delilah said. Disappointment painted her voice. "I am to be your wife in name only."

"You are my wife."

"How can you say this? You spend so little time with me, you know nothing about me. And I know nothing of you."

Samson calmed. Delilah thought she saw tenderness creep into his face. "I…" he began.

"You insist that I am not your prisoner but your wife." Samson nodded agreement. "What wife knows nothing of her husband? What woman has not even been bedded by him?" She looked wistfully and hopefully at him. "Three moons have passed and you have not rhetorical X ratatouille

touched me as a man touches his wife. Is there something wrong with me? Do I not please you, or perhaps you do not like women?"

Samson's nose flared open in disgust. "I am not that sort of man, and you should know it by now."

"Oh, I have heard about your skills with the temple prostitutes. But did you think that I was just like them? That I was eager to mate with the all-powerful Samson?" Delilah stared at Samson down her slender golden nose. "I had dreams before you came and stole me from my family. I was to be the Priestess of El – the Sacred Anointed One." She took a breath to steady herself. "It would have been my duty to lead the temple in offerings to the God. Mine the honor of saying the Sacred Seven." She stood proudly before him. "You are not the only one who serves his God. And I serve them still."

Samson silenced her with a glare as he towered over her. "You know what will happen if I should find another shrine to your El."

"Yes, I know, Samson." Delilah said defiantly. "Do not fear; I will not embarrass you with having a shrine to a foreign god where your people can see it."

"Not just where they cannot see it, Delilah. I will not allow it to be anywhere in my home."

Delilah saw a shadow shift behind a curtain. Umi's withered brown foot stuck out below.

"You have held me hostage long enough, Samson. If you will not set me free from this mockery of a marriage, then I must return to my people." Delilah looked at him, unblinking. "And do not think that I will not. I know that you need this peace as much as my people do.

"You have said too much. Be silent or I will strike you."

"You are a coward," Delilah taunted.

With a swiftness that belied his muscular body, Samson raised his hand and struck Delilah across the face. Just as swiftly, he fell to the ground as his body began to twitch uncontrollably. Delilah held her hand to her cheek and watched with concern. The spasm seemed to be over, she thought, and she squatted beside him. Another tremor took Samson, his body shivered and shook. His arm struck her. She shouted for help. She kept a safe distance while she waited. Soon Delilah heard the sound of bare feet slapping against the marble floors. Umi ran in, Zeev came behind her.

"Has he begun this again?" asked Zeev.

"What do you mean when you say again?" asked Delilah. The three stood and watched as Samson shook anew.

"I will tell you more when we have settled him," Zeev declared. "Now we must make certain that he does not hurt himself." He looked at Delilah; the red mark on her cheek blazed. "Or anyone else."

"How," Delilah asked. Samson was powerful. Strong. She didn't understand what was happening. Samson stopped shaking. He laid quiet on the floor. Still.

"I will move him to somewhere safe," Zeev said, as he grasped Samson by the arm and carried his still form out of the hall. "I will stay with him until he wakes."

Delilah nodded her acceptance, and turned to Umi. Umi reached a hand to Delilah's cheek.

"What did I say, foolish child. See, now he has struck you."

"Yes," Delilah said. "But I am not certain that he meant to do it. Find calendula; it will soothe and heal this."

"Of course."

Delilah waited. She expected Zeev to arrive any moment to tell her that Samson had awakened from his episode. She paced the balcony. Umi left her alone. Too restless to wait any longer, she entered Samson's chambers. Zeev stood rigidly beside the bed though his eyes were half closed. She laid a hand on his shoulder to rouse him. He jerked awake and spun away from her.

"Has nothing changed?" Delilah asked.

"Nothing," Zeev answered.

"Go sleep then. I will keep watch," she said. Zeev regarded her carefully. "I will have Umi wake you if anything should change." Zeev nodded acceptance. "Before you go, please tell me what you mean that this has happened before."

Zeev looked at Samson and then at Delilah. He sighed and began. "It was after his first marriage. The bride's parents would not wait for Samson to consummate the marriage, and gave her to another. Samson," he paused, "Samson became enraged and killed the entire family. It was a moon before he stopped with these fits. All that time, he could not be with us and our families. He was unclean. Then the elders sent him to the desert, so he could be purified. When he returned, a prophet came and cleansed him. The illness left him with a great strength that he brought into battle. He was allowed to become a warrior for our God, blessed by our priests. If he has become unclean again…" Zeev shook his head.

"Thank you, Zeev," Delilah nodded as he turned and left the room. She found a cushion and a place to support her back against the wall, and watched Samson as he lay resting. He seemed peaceful now. Gentle, even. He murmured something unintelligible.

"What did you say, Samson?" she asked. He answered her with silence. Perhaps, she thought, he would like someone to talk to. "Would you like to hear about my life, then?" He grunted and turned his body toward her. She took it as a sign. "Let me tell you about my mother," she began.

*

"For your cheek, Delilah," Umi said. Delilah woke with a start. She rubbed sleep from her eyes.

"Oh, Umi," Delilah said as she inhaled the delicate fruity scent. She smelled something else, a little bitter and earthy.

"I found arnica too; it will hide the bruise and help it fade faster."

Delilah watched Zeev as he stood in the doorway. He studied Umi applying the salve to her skin.

"Zeev, I am so glad that you are here."

"I cannot stay," Zeev said.

"What do you mean, you cannot stay. You must stay. You are his friend."

"If I stay, I will become unclean. You are Philistine. What do you care of that? Nothing. I must go to the priests and be prepared for cleansing or I cannot share in the offering this month."

Samson began to thrash against the pillows. He rocked from side to side. His arms flailed wildly. Delilah looked uncertainly at Zeev.

"So you will leave me to this alone?"

"You have your slave," he answered coldly. "She will help you."

"Please, Zeev," Delilah implored. "Stay. Help me. I am asking you as his wife." Zeev stared at Samson who had now come to lie still once again.

"Perhaps if we tie him he will not harm himself or you."

"What could we use that could hold him?"

"My captain has told me there are new thongs in the armory. If we tie him with those maybe he will not be able to break free."

"Umi, run to the armory," Delilah commanded.

"No," Zeev insisted, "I will go. Tend to her bruises." He slipped into the hallways and disappeared.

*

Samson was bound now. So long as the thongs were kept oiled, they did not dry or harden. They held Samson onto the bed, where he could not thrash He seemed to be resting peacefully. Delilah stayed by his side much of her day and all of her nights.

She passed water through his lips, bathed him with a rough cloth, and anointed his body with healing oils. Delilah felt embarrassed that this was the first opportunity she had to get to know her husband. Awkward at first, she slowly became familiar with the contrasts of his body; the coarseness of his fingers, hands and feet, the smoothness of his muscular arms and legs, the firmness of his chest. She grew accustomed to the sound of his rumblings as he rested. His thoughts were a mystery that she had yet to unfold. Perhaps, she mused, when he was well she could learn more about him. Every once in a while, Samson would mumble something incoherent and then fall swiftly back into slumber. At these times, she spoke to Samson, telling him of her home, her family, and her escapades as a child until fatigue overwhelmed her.

Samson stirred then and shouted unintelligibly.

"I wish I could understand you," Delilah said. She bent over Samson, listening to his muttering. She laid her head upon his chest and listened to the steady beating of his heart. His earthy smell enveloped her and soon sleep overtook her.

*

What is Uncle Achaziah doing here, Delilah thought, looking about the chamber. Samson lay motionless on the cushions, sleeping and bound in the leather thongs. Achaziah, on the other hand, was advancing.

"Now we will be rid of this atrocity," he shouted as he motioned to the soldiers that had come with him. "No more will you have to submit to a lesser man." He directed the soldiers, dressed in leathers and helms, to surround Samson and Delilah. They drew their swords, and holding them before them, they crept toward the bed.

"Samson," Delilah whispered, "Wake now. Defend yourself." He laid inert, deep in sleep as he had been for some weeks now. "Samson," she spoke, "you are in danger. Awaken!" Samson's eyes twitched open briefly and then closed. They may kill me too, Delilah feared, if I cannot rouse Samson. Summoning the voice she used in temple for the petitions to the god, Delilah shouted "Samson, the Philistines are upon you!"

*

Delilah jerked awake when she fell onto the floor. She rubbed her aching bottom as she watched Samson. He slept. But the thongs that had held him all these weeks were snapped cleanly in two. Too drowsy from a week of watchfulness, Delilah mumbled something about caring for it in the morning. She laid her head on Samson's shoulder. She fell asleep.

CHAPTER 7

Delilah watched as a slave dipped a cloth into a cool basin of water and raised it to Umi's lips. Umi lay naked and sweating, thrashing on her pallet. Delilah raised a silent prayer of thanks to her gods. Although she had endured mild symptoms of nausea and vomiting and cramping for a day or so, the slaves in Samson's household had suffered from this plague for more than four days. Some succumbed; their bodies were borne away by their own. Samson too, writhed with pain. Delilah did all she could to ease his torment. She conceded that there was nothing she could do but restrain him so that he could not hurt himself or others with his violent spasms. Thankfully, there had been new ropes near the spring. Still wet, they smelled like the hemp plant they'd been made of. She brought him fresh water and dried flat bread to ease his symptoms. Her efforts were slowly being rewarded. Samson no longer heaved his meals up no sooner than he had swallowed them.

That is the last time that I let Umi cook a meal, Delilah thought as she stripped out of her linen robes and stood in the darkness of the servants' quarters. If only Umi hadn't made that goat dish, none of us would be suffering from this new plague. She pulled Umi's yellow woollen robe over her head and tried to adjust it to obscure her physique. She slipped Umi's grass slippers on her feet and ambled away from the mountain top she called home.

The robe dragged, catching on rocks and roots. The cloth scraped her skin, making her itch. Her every step felt prickly and sharp.

Oh mighty El, she prayed, see how your daughter is brought low. As you did in the beginning, bring order from chaos. Bring justice. She stopped herself before she continued the ritual exhortations. What am I doing? Can El truly hear me here, among the Israelites? I am but one drop of water in the mighty river. I am but a speck of dirt on the mountain of my god. How can he still hear me without the charms and oils and incense?

The well came within view, and the fetid smell of the business conducted there rose up to meet her. Delilah trod toward the market place, following the mewling, clucking, and bawling of the livestock.

A haggard-looking man stood there. He spoke loudly to those gathered nearby. A holy man, Delilah guessed, from the way he was talking. His presence might mean trouble for her if she wasn't careful. Someone might recognize her.

Some of the villagers were conducting their business of buying and selling near the well. Some stood listening attentively to the wild man. A woman with a rounded belly held a basket of eggs in one arm and held a stick laced with several limp-necked chickens. A man next to her kept one eye on the sheep he had brought for sale and the other on the holy man.

The woman patted her belly protectively. "The Prophet has returned!"

"What is he preaching today?"

"Something about belonging to God."

Her companion shook his head, and clucked to convince his sheep to stay nearby. "I fed him last time, sister. It is your turn today."

The woman nodded and approached the wild man. He smiled at her as she gave him two chickens. He lashed them to a rope around his waist. He looked past the woman; Delilah felt his gaze fall on her.

Delilah pulled her head into her hood, wishing she could disappear. Hiding inside her robes, she stepped on the long hem and fell to the dry packed earth. Her empty basket flipped out of her hands and over her head. A couple turned to stare at her and swiftly turned away. Delilah darted a hand out through the long sleeves, trying to gather her skirts so that they would not trip her. She hoisted on the top half of her robe, trying to shorten the skirt and pulled too hard. The hem of the skirts rose above her knees. Delilah dropped to her knees and tugged on the hem until it seemed to touch her ankles. She would have crawled away, back the way she came, except that a sheep had blocked her retreat.

The crust covered man had hopped onto the white stones of the well. Three men scrambled into action, surrounding him, preventing him from falling in.

"You," he pointed wildly, "Who are you?"

Delilah looked around, her mind felt jumbled as the broken rocks. Was he talking to her? She looked where he pointed. He was talking to her, she decided. She began to crouch into a ball in an effort to avoid the villager's stares.

The man leapt from one white stone to the next, despite the protests of those next to him. He scrambled down off the edge of the well and scampered toward her. He squatted before her and pushed back the cloth around her hair. His smell filled her nose; Delilah felt bile rise in her throat. He was soiled and dirty. Delilah tried to turn and hide.

He touched her shoulder and turned her to face him.

"Who are you?"

"No one." Delilah shoved the sheep out of her way and began to walk away from the marketplace. He followed.

"You are not who you say you are."

"I tell you, I am no one important."

"But that is where you are wrong. You are of God!"

Delilah sighed in frustration.

"And because you are of God, everything you do is of God."

"I do nothing," she shouted over her shoulder.

"Wrong again! Your every breath is the breath of God. Your every footstep is God's footstep on this earth. This very earth is of God. You walk on God, dance on God, eat on God, even sleep on God."

Delilah hurried her pace away from the prophet and stubbed her toe on a rock in her path. She winced as she rubbed it. She looked and saw that the well and the busy marketplace were behind them.

"Here, let me help you," he said gently, extending his hand.

"There is no help for me." She refused him, and sat upon a rock outcropping a short distance away.

"Who is your husband?"

She stared at her feet and muttered. "I have no husband."

"You lie. Your husband is God."

"Then God is a terrible husband and I want nothing of him."

"God is your father."

"I have no father or mother. I am an orphan," Delilah insisted. "I am alone."

"God is my father and my mother," the prophet affirmed.

"Both? How can that be so?"

"God is."

"You have a peculiar god." Delilah felt her lips draw into a half smile.

"Perhaps," he answered, "but no different than yours."

"You know nothing of my god," Delilah argued.

"I know your god as well as my own. Does God not answer your prayers, listen to your laments?"

"I do not know." Delilah tumbled his question in her mind. If my mind and heart are focused on the god, he must still hear me. El has always listened to my prayers, offered me solace when my mother died, gave me strength when the testing began, solved the puzzle of justice when the merchant Talten had tried to steal her father's ancestral property. "Perhaps," Delilah answered to the rocks and fields. She was alone. Oh no, she realized, the day is almost done and I have bought nothing at market. Turning around, she almost tripped over the rock beside her. Her basket sat there; a chicken hung its limp neck over the lip. Lifting it, she found a cup filled with some dates and some tubers. The Prophet, she thought, and raised a prayer of thanks. It isn't what she had gone to market for. But with some ingenuity, it would suffice.

CHAPTER 8

The slippery skin of the roasted chicken slid down Delilah's throat. She sucked on the moist meat, seasoned with lemon and sage, and let it linger on her tongue.

"I have decided," Samson announced, "that I no longer wish to be a fighter."

She nursed on a chicken bone, trying to draw the succulent juices into her mouth. "What would you do then?"

"I do not know. It is all I have ever known. My parents so wanted a child that they promised Jehovah that I would be raised as a Nazirite, and given back to him as a gift."

"You were sacrificed to your god?" Delilah sucked on the chicken bone again, this time too hard. A piece flew into her windpipe. She choked then coughed it out. What sort of god would demand this of his people?

"No, Delilah. I was given to his service even before I was born. So I was kept apart." Delilah furrowed her brow and listened as Samson continued. "Boys my age were taught to care for the sheep; I spent my time learning warfare and weapons. Of course, it meant that I could not play with the other children. I was so strong that I would harm them playing a simple game of catch. Wrestling was out of the question. I almost killed another child when I was three years old." Samson sipped from his cup. "After that, none of the children would come near me. I was truly alone. I could only eat meat that was clean. My parents took care of me, made certain that I ate the blessed foods, kept holy, and listened to the holy words of my teachers. When I became a young man, my parents could no longer control the power I had, so they sent me to the elders, who offered me a chance to develop my skill and let me learn how to fight." Samson laid the cup down before him.

"When they saw me fight they believed that they had a giant among them, and that Yahweh blessed them. They asked me to fight. So I fought for them. I went from one campaign to another. I was a warrior through and through."

"What has changed you now? Why would you give up the life you have known?

"I thought I was fighting for myself. But I was really just fighting for them. Now I have something that I value more." He looked at her and Delilah thought she saw longing in his eyes.

"If you will not fight, what will you do then?"

"Perhaps I would become a sheep farmer like my cousins."

Delilah laughed. "The mighty Samson a sheep farmer?

Samson raised his cup to his lips. He took a drink. "I've drunk from this cup forty times forty. I've been what everyone wanted me to be. I've given my life to my god and my people. First as a warrior, then as a judge." Delilah watched as Samson turned the cup in his hands. "I have lived apart, alone. But now I have found something to belong to." He looked up and smiled at Delilah. "I want to be like any man, content in my home with my wife and children to surround me. I want to celebrate the birth of my son and help him learn the kaddash. I can't do that if I am dead in a field of battle. For once, I want to just be... Samson."

"That's all you have ever been to me," Delilah answered. "But how can you just walk away from your life as a warrior?"

"My strength belongs to Jehovah. I am only strong because of the agreement my parents made and that I took up upon becoming a man."

"Your agreement? What do you mean?"

"When I was sent to the desert, I purified my body for forty days and nights. I fasted and drank little. I removed all my body hair and for the first time in my life, I was weak as a newborn lamb. When the prophet came and saw that I had made my peace with JHVH, he brought me to temple and declared me cleansed. That was when I took the vow to be a Nazirite."

Delilah shook her head in confusion.

"I swore that I would serve my God and as a sign of my covenant with him that I would not cut my hair. Ever. I can brush it and comb it and oil it and tie it, but never cut it. If I were to do so, my strength would flow away from me like snowmelt from the top of a mountain."

A sound of pottery falling and breaking upset the quiet of the room. A shard slipped under a curtain against the wall and across the hard floor. Umi scrambled from behind the curtain. A frown came over Samson's face and he swiftly rose from his seat to confront her.

"What were you doing back there? Were you spying on us perhaps?" he asked.

Umi began to stutter a response as Delilah came to see what the problem was. Delilah drew back the curtain. A coconut lay upon a small table, surrounded with small shells. It was as she had feared. "Umi!" she admonished.

"What is this?" Samson bellowed. "A shrine to a foreign god in my house?" Umi nodded slowly and backed into Delilah.

"What did I tell you about this?" Samson's face turned a deep red. "No shrines! Not one!" He began to swing his arms, as he had the morning that he had struck Delilah.

Seeing danger, Delilah stepped in front of Umi. "Samson," she began, "calm yourself..." Delilah spoke too late. Samson swung his hand and connected with something that was both soft and hard. There was a cracking sound. Delilah doubled over in pain.

"Delilah!" Samson shouted; his face suddenly white. He bent over her, a look of concern on his face. Samson turned to Umi and shouted. "Do not just stand there; get the physician." Umi scuttled out of the room.

Samson laid Delilah gently on her bed. Delilah felt an excruciating pain in her side. The physician bustled into the room, carrying a small box of ointments and herbs. He made her lie upon her bed and patted and prodded her abdomen. When he reached the base of her ribs, Delilah howled in pain.

"You have a cracked rib," he declared. "I can only give you something for the pain while it heals." He mixed some vile-smelling plants in a rock bowl and ground them. Taking a pinch of them, he put them into a cup; he poured wine into it, raised it to her lips and bade her to drink. Delilah coughed upon tasting the bitter concoction.

"It will help you rest," the physician said.

Zeev ran into the room. "Samson, the war council is meeting now, and as commander of the army, you must come!"

"But Delilah is hurt," Samson protested. "I cannot leave her alone!"

"I will stay and keep watch over her," the physician offered. "I will need to stay to ensure that she is not in too much pain and there are no other complications."

Delilah watched Samson as he turned first one way, then the other. "Go, Samson," she whispered. He bent down to Delilah, his eyes full of concern for her. "Do what you must."

Samson nodded and gently caressed her cheek. "I will return soon," he assured her. Delilah smiled drowsily as she watched Samson and Zeev disappear. Her thoughts tumbled like rocks down a mountainside.

Delilah walked side by side with Samson to the sound of the zarb and a zurna. The sound of a drum came from a distance, like the drum for a funeral procession. Her cousins' funeral, she remembered. Uncle Achaziah's face rose before her, gaunt with grief, his words echoing in her mind. "Discover how to kill him," he said. Here it is, then, Delilah knew it. Cut Samson's hair and he will be weak. Should she do it? Should she betray him? Her cheek stung from the slap she had received at Samson's hand. Bitterness crept through her, anger at his violence. She tasted the dust from the broken image of El.

Her body throbbed with an ache deep in her core. It wasn't as if she and Samson were truly husband and wife. They still had not consummated their marriage. Delilah's heart soured at the thought that perhaps she never would. What if her wound proved fatal? Samson may not be a perfect husband, but he tried to be a good one the best he knew. There was a soft side of him, one that cared about her. A side that was weak, that she could nurture and care for; a part of him that needed her. He even had a bath put in for me, Delilah remembered. The warmth of it would be welcome now, she thought, her body felt chilled. God of Justice, guide me, she silently implored. My family demands one answer, my promise to my husband demands another. Guide me, Great Arbiter. Her body felt heavy, her eyelids closed.

It was half-dark when Delilah opened her eyes. The physician had left, but where was Samson? Where was Umi? Delilah called for Umi, but she did not come. Delilah tried to rise, but her ribs ached too much. She slumped back to her bed, pain racking her body. Where is everyone, she thought? Why does no one answer me? A sound came from the darkness then. A shadow emerged from the darkness and approached the bed. Something glinted in the glow from the moonlight. It was an angry looking blade.

CHAPTER 9

Delilah drew in a breath and whimpered in pain. She touched her hand to her ribcage. A thousand tiny knives seemed to pierce her. She yelped. Someone, she could sense, was in the room.

"Umi?" she asked as she forced her eyes open. Samson stood before her. His bloody hands held a warriors' knife before him. She screamed. The knife clattered to the stone floor. He stooped and gently caressed Delilah.

"Hush, Delilah, be at peace, the physician will come soon."

Delilah took a breath and shook. "What are you doing, Samson?"

"I have come to ask your help."

"My help? How can I help you?"

"I need you. I can not bear this." Silence hung between them like a veil.

"They have turned their backs on me. I cannot leave offerings at temple. I cannot bathe in the baths, I cannot fight ... I am an outcast." He lay his bloodied hands before her. Where his thumbs should have been were blackened sores.

Delilah felt bile rise up her throat. "What have they done to you?" she cried, taking his hands in hers.

"They said that if I do not go to war against your people again, I will not be allowed to remain here. They will send us into the desert. I cannot go to war again."

"You have always been a warrior, Samson, why not now?"

"Because I would be breaking my oath to you. I have broken too many promises. I have failed YHVH and I have failed you. Let me keep just one promise. I must make restitution for this, and there is only one way that I know." His fingers wrapped around the knife handle; he pushed it into her hand. "You must cut my hair, Delilah."

"But without your hair, you will be weak."

"No," Samson shook his head, "for once, I will be strong. I will honor you as I should have from the start. I swore to keep you safe, and my own fist has struck you; my power has hurt you. You must cut my hair."

"What will you do when you are no longer a warrior?"

"I will work as other men work. I will have sheep and fowl. I will keep my house. I will love my wife and help raise our children." He paused. "Yes, and to make sure that I cannot change my mind once you have begun, I have brought these ropes." He dragged a chair before her bed. "Tie me in this chair so that I cannot leave," he said. Delilah sat up; she winced at the pain in her chest. She held her breath as Samson sat facing away from her and grasped his hands behind the back of the chair. The cord was coarse and wiry in her hands; she wound it around his wrists. She groaned with the effort of tying the rope.

"Are you ready?" she asked as she heaved a sigh. The only answer she heard was the murmur Samson made as he spoke his prayers to his god.

Delilah picked up the knife in one hand, and considered it carefully. She thought of the knife in her dream. The blade shone dangerously in the half-light of her room. With her other hand, she drew Samson's hair taut and brought the knife near. She felt him tense before her and knew what she must do.

Delilah yanked the blade upward through Samson's wiry hair. A chunk of dark hair fell to the floor. A shout erupted from Samson.

"Hallelujah!" he sobbed.

"I will stop," Delilah offered.

"Complete the work," he begged.

Delilah obliged, and cried along with his sobs with each fresh cut. She dropped the blade into the pile of hair on the floor. "I can do no more," she said.

"Then release me and look upon me with kindness, my wife."

Delilah carefully unwound the ropes and, exhausted, lay back upon her bed. Samson shook his tunic; hair flew to meet what was already cut. He stripped out of his tunic and lay next to her. It felt strange and uncomfortable, but pleasant, Delilah thought. She looked into his eyes. He smiled.

"Why are you smiling? I could have killed you."

"No, you could not," Samson shook his head. "You are too gentle to kill another. I have slaughtered children." He frowned and then sighed. "I do not deserve you."

Delilah laughed. "You are a good man, Samson."

"A good man, you say. I say I am just a man now. Not a warrior, not a judge, just Samson."

"Just Samson." Delilah nodded. "I am just Delilah." She saw his expression of concern as she winced in pain.

"Let me get the physician for you," Samson offered, starting to rise.

"No, stay here Samson. Soon enough, the world will come to make its demands of us. But for now we are just Samson and Delilah." She saw a smile break across his face.

"That is all I have wished for."

"Tonight you have your wish, and I, mine. Hold me?" she asked.

He embraced her tenderly so as not to harm her. He traced spirals upon her shoulders and down her back. He tipped her head upwards to his and looked into her eyes. His eyes looked like glowing embers. He covered her lips with his. Her body buzzed like the bees at blossom time in the orchard. She felt sleepy and awake; a jumble of emotions. All she felt was his body against hers. She marveled at how their bodies seemed to fit so perfectly together. She felt his excitement against her; her breath caught with her own exhilaration.

Was this what it was like between husband and wife she wondered. She laid down again. He touched her belly, her breasts, her thighs. Where his fingers touched, his lips and tongue soon followed. She burned to know what the mystery was of the joining she had so often heard of. Samson looked to her imploringly. She nodded.

The slap of feet on the stone floor woke Delilah as the sun's light peeked into their chamber. She marveled at the sight and the feeling of her arms and legs entangled with Samson's.

"Commander, they are here," a voice called out.

"Seize him," Achaziah said.

Delilah's eyes grew wide as she shook Samson and screamed in terror.

"We are besieged!"

Samson startled awake, and readied to fight. The Philistine guard pounced on him, grabbing his wrists and pinning him to the ground. Delilah tried to rise, but fell, gripping her ribs and crying in agony.

"Well done, Delilah," Achaziah said. He grinned. "You have delivered Samson to us, as promised. It is only fitting that you should be paid for your suffering." He untied a bag from his waist and tossed it to where Delilah lay. It split; silver coins scattered across the floor.

"No," Delilah cried, "do not take him!"

"There is no need for you to pretend love any longer, Delilah," Achaziah said. He stooped and examined her; alarm flashed across his face when he saw her injury. "We will take care of him." He paused. "Physician!" he shouted; a man approached her. "Tend to my niece and bring her home. She has suffered enough already." He turned and left the room. "Bring the prisoner," Achaziah commanded. Samson struggled in vain. The guard led him from the chamber into the dawn light.

The physician looked into Delilah's eyes. He poked and prodded her ribs and back.

"All is not lost dear," he said. "We can mend you."

Delilah's heart ached like it was breaking. Why did she feel that this was something that might not ever be repaired?

CHAPTER 10

Two moons had passed since the night that Samson had been captured by Uncle Achaziah. It seemed to Delilah like a lifetime ago, a lifetime spent wandering the desert in her dreams, searching for her husband and her place.

Two moons of lying still, her mind wandering where her body could not. Time and rest had made her body strong; but her heart felt bruised and achy. Her thoughts ran to Samson, she dreamt him, smelled him, tasted him and their last moments together. They ran over and over in her head, like the songs of the praise that she had once intoned at the base of the god's image.

For two moons, she watched the life of her father's household buzz around her. She felt dizzy from watching the spinning of the servants, and anxious to be free of her confines. She began with daily offerings and prayers to her gods. Her days were filled with the rituals she had learned from Samson and those of her own, the rituals of rising and bathing, the rituals of dressing and eating. She felt her father's disapproving look upon her with every bow and song. Delilah didn't dare tell him that she could not imagine herself as a priestess of El any longer. How could she, now that she had come to know another path, another god. Not that she wanted to worship Samson's god. No, his god was too strict for her, too foreign. Yet she remembered the words of the Prophet, who had admonished her to resume her prayers once more. She heard every whisper of the servants who ministered to her body, while she ministered to her mind and soul.

Delilah was determined to walk before the physician had counseled. Every day since the last new moon she had ventured further from her chamber. Every day she grew in strength. She had to learn what had come of her husband. Delilah decided that it was time to venture out of her sanctuary. Relief washed over her at the news that the Oracle had sent a response to her request for audience. She was welcome to call upon him— but first she had to get permission from her father. That would only be accomplished if she could endure sitting through a meal with Uncle Achaziah.

Since her return home, Achaziah had become a permanent resident in her father's palace. His home, he claimed, seemed too empty without his sons to keep him company.

Delilah didn't know if she had the strength to sit close to Achaziah without wanting to kill him. He was the man who had captured her husband; the man who, if the tales were to be believed, had killed Samson before even returning home. No, Delilah decided, if Samson had died in prison, Achaziah would have paraded his body through the streets. For the crime of killing his sons, Achaziah would have devised a crueler torture for Samson. Her heart ached to think it.

Samson was forgotten to all but her. Father never spoke of him, nor asked about her life among the Israelites. Uncle Achaziah avoided all talk of him.

"The Oracle has agreed to see for us," Delilah said between bites. "I would like to go see him today."

"Of course," her father said, "I know he has been a friend for many years." He paused. "You know that you have been offered a position at temple when you are ready."

"Yes Father," she answered, "but my heart is too heavy to sing the exaltations of El." She rose slowly from her seat "Still, I must go make offerings at the temple for our fig harvest and I have need of the Oracle's wisdom about the problem with our almonds."

"There is a litter ready to bear you when you are prepared," Achaziah offered.

"Thank you, Uncle. I wish however to walk," Delilah replied.

"Let me have a guard escort you; you would have to pass through the marketplace and I could not bear it if you were hurt."

Delilah held her belly as her stomach gave an uncertain lurch. Was Uncle trying to protect me the way he was unable to protect his sons or is he suspicious of me and what I might do she wondered. "Thank you, Uncle, but I have already arranged it with the temple. The Acolyte to the Priestess will walk with me and help me prepare to enter into the presence of the god and his oracle." She looked for signs of Achaziah's displeasure. Either Uncle was unmoved or very skillful at hiding his feelings. She couldn't tell. "I must go now, for she will arrive soon." She turned away from the table and stepped out toward the terrace. The almond trees were covered in tiny buds, while the fig trees lay dormant. Was this an omen?

"She hasn't been the same since her imprisonment," she heard her father say to Achaziah. "I worry for her."

"As do I," she heard Achaziah reply. "As do I."

*

Delilah's heart leapt into her throat at the sight of him. Blind from birth, his pink eyes stared blankly back at her from under a shock of white hair. He was covered in the white gowns of his station, seated before the image of the god. Delilah laid a cone of frankincense upon the glowing ember in the brazier before him. Sweet pungent smoke enveloped them. Delilah smiled in spite of herself. For the first time since the day that Samson had entered her life, she felt some measure of comfort.

"Great One," Delilah bowed reverently to him and touched her forehead to the smooth stone floor.

"Rest in the presence of the god," the Oracle intoned.

"I trust in El and in his counsel," she responded in a singsong.

"The god is just and wise," the Oracle chanted, "He sees all and rules all and Justice is his name."

"All praise be to El," Delilah sang. The chants and prayers buoyed up her heart and the questions that burned inside her. She stilled her mind, closed her eyes and sat in silence while she waited for the Oracle's proclamation.

"You are a terrible liar, Delilah," the Oracle laughed. "Why did you tell your father that I would predict the harvest when you know full well that I cannot?"

"You are the Oracle," Delilah teased her friend. "Tell me what I truly need to know."

The Oracle chewed thoughtfully on a leaf and took several deep, even breaths. He hummed a melody and then fell silent.

"Your family betrayed you and has returned to the source. El's justice will be their reward."

Delilah nodded. Her father had already told her of Umi's hand in the capture of Samson, how Umi had gone first to the Israelite physician;

how she had hidden near their room and watched as Delilah cut Samson's hair, then slipped away to her father's home. How Umi had told Uncle that Samson was weak and now was the time to strike. How Umi had asked for safe passage back to her people and disappeared. Bile rose in Delilah's throat at the thought of her betrayal.

"The god waits for you to fulfill your destiny; to serve your god and your people."

Delilah frowned. She didn't want to be reminded of the role that awaited her. Her time among the Israelites had changed her. It wasn't as if she felt drawn to the Israelite god, or that she felt repulsed by him. Through the Prophet and Samson, she had come to see that both her god and Samson's god were much the same, both divine parents to their people. She couldn't imagine having to explain this to the Priests of El. No, Delilah decided as she felt her stomach harden, she would not tell them. They would not understand.

"Your husband," the Oracle said, "is dead."

Delilah wailed. She hugged her belly as she doubled up in pain. "No!" she cried.

"The Oracle has spoken," an attendant whispered.

"The god is justice and wisdom," Delilah responded. Her words felt far from her, dry as the desert and cold as stone. Is this why I have not dreamed of Samson, she wondered? Ever since the night of the arrest, she had been unable to see him, although she asked El for visions of him. Her dreams drifted in sand. Delilah felt lost, cast out on the desert. She felt hands holding her gently, cleaning her with scented cloths. Attendants came and bore her into the sanctuary of the god and helped her lie down on a mat. They anointed her with oils and left her in the silence and lamplight to take in presence of the god. Delilah's thoughts bubbled inside her like the contents of her stomach.

She looked upon the image of El; his once comforting face seemed severe. Delilah bowed before him and prayed. She sat back on her feet, knees splayed and toes curled under her. Delilah laid her arms upon her thighs, surrendering herself to El.

"Help me," she sobbed. She bowed before the statue. She closed her eyes and sang a lament for Samson. The melody sounded like the familiar mourning songs of her people, yet different. Chants of the Israelite priests wove themselves into her familiar song. Delilah felt the melody twine, build and fall. Her mind followed the droning, humming in her chest. She slipped into trance and waited for her god to speak as he had before, a roaring voice in the wind. A figure took form before her.

"Daughter," it said, "save your husband."

CHAPTER 11

Delilah lurched. Her head felt light, but her limbs felt heavy, as if walking through honey. One thought filled her mind. "I must find Samson." She stood and walked out of the Oracle's Sanctuary and through the Temple of El. Priests and priestesses, servants and acolytes were busy preparing for the annual flowering festival. Their attention was turned to Ashtoresh, the serpent goddess and mother. The hissing sound of their systrum sent a shiver down her spine; the droning of their chant buzzed inside her.

Delilah moved in silence through the temple and down the stairs uninterrupted. Her footsteps took her through the marketplace, now empty in the midday heat. The affluent families would be sitting in their chaises by the river, where the breezes were strong and servants would wave feathered fans to cool them. Their homes were in the same scale as the temples; imposing and impressive, meant to keep the peasant class subservient. A sweeper sat idle next to the brush he used to clear refuse from the stone walks. Her footsteps took her through the peasant quarters. Here, the path turned to packed earth. Delilah walked past the well, normally a hub of activity; it was bare except for the solitary beggar who lounged in the corner near The Wall.

The Wall divided the peasant quarters from the slave section of the city. It also acted as an entrance to the jail. During the midday heat, even the guards were resting in the dark coolness. The presence of the god hung over Delilah. She walked through the entrance to the jail without confrontation. Her feet led her through the dusty streets. Children with barely a rag to cover them scuttled into the cool shade of the crumbling buildings at her passage. She paused, at last, in a dark passage off a deserted side street. Here, the tall walls of the jail were a startling contrast to the broken buildings of the slaves. Here, Delilah stopped. A man held a spear in front of him and stepped forward.

It was the same soldier who had taken Samson prisoner two moons before. She watched him first react to her appearance, then to the symbols of her status. She observed that he had recognized her.

"Daughter of El," he began, "you do not belong here."

"You have jailed my husband," Delilah asserted. "I have come to see him."

"He is offal," the solider said. "You deserve a real man, not an animal." He put his spear aside and pressed her against the wall. She grit her teeth and tried to push him away from her.

"I deserve to see my husband," Delilah whispered. "Unless you want to explain to the Priests the wrong you committed against the god's own, I suggest you remove yourself from me now." She glowered at him. He knew, just as well as she did, that the punishment for assaulting the god's servants would render him a guest of the very place he guarded.

The soldier leapt away from her, as if her skin was a poison to be avoided. He snatched up his spear. "Samson is that way, you may see him if you can find him," he pointed into the semi-darkness.

Delilah followed a passage way that grew damp and warm the further she went. Her head grew dizzy from the heat that permeated the jail. As she passed, she could see that the prisoners were encased in cages of stone and metal. Their emaciated bodies stank of feces and urine. She tried hard not to look, but gruesome fascination and grim determination made her look in each chamber. Which one held Samson? Would she know him? Would he know her?

The prisoners taunted her with ribald jeers. Delilah was deaf to them. One man was silent. Delilah stopped and examined him. His body was withered from starvation; his muscles were stringy looking from hard work. Angry red welts ran in strips upon his back. There were blisters on his shoulders where the yoke had been put upon him. His hair grew in short patches on his head.

"Stop staring at me," the man shouted.

"I am sorry," she said. "I seek my husband. His name is Samson. Do you know him?"

"I know him," the man answered. He turned to face the bars and Delilah. "I am he."

Oozing red gashes were where Samson's eyes once were. Delilah felt his wounds as if they were hers. Her eyes wept in sympathy and pain. She fell to her knees beside the cell, crying for him to come. Samson lurched toward her. Delilah tried to embrace him through the bars.

"Let me take care of you," Delilah whimpered. She caressed his soiled and blooded body with her hair and her tears. Samson pushed her away.

"You betrayed me to my enemies!" he yelled.

"No, Samson, I swear, I did not betray you."

Samson hurled himself at his cell wall. 'Liar," he called out.

"No, I tell you truth, Samson," Delilah rebutted. "It was not I." She sighed; then frowned. "It was Umi. She knew your weakness. She knew your violence. She sought only to protect me."

"At my cost?"

"At any cost, Samson. She is gone. The desert take her," she swore.

"Amen," they swore together. Samson's rage seemed to leave him. He sat against the stone wall, and spoke into the darkness.

"I am less than a worm. My god has forsaken me. My wife has left me. I am alone."

"Samson, no," Delilah pled, "I am your wife. I love you. Your god loves you."

"How can my god love me if he leaves me to rot in this place?"

"Did not the prophet speak of the love of your god, how he would care for you as well as he cares for a bird or the lilies of the field?"

"It changes nothing, Delilah," he grumbled."I am still here, caught like a lamb in the thicket, trapped in this prison."

"The only prison you have is one of your own making."

"Then release me, Delilah. Help me die. I cannot bear this any longer."

"I will not. How can you speak of this abomination?"

"You made this prison for me. You, your father, and your uncle. Now I will never see the Kingdom of Heaven."

"Samson, let me help you."

"There is no help for me," Samson yelled as he hurled a rock toward the bars and Delilah. "Go away from me!" It skittered, ricocheting against the bars. The noise reverberated through the chamber. "Begone!" he shouted. He rained rocks and curses upon her and her family.

Delilah leapt out of reach of his throw. His words bruised her heart. She ached as she turned to run down the corridor toward the exit. She realized that her husband was lost to her. She wanted to run home and seek her father's comfort. Instead, Achaziah stood in her way, a brace of guards beside him.

"Delilah, you have come at the just time," he said. He faced the guards and commanded them. "Bind him tightly; he must not escape." They burst into Samson's cell and grasped him. They bound him hand and foot, and dragged him out of his cell. Samson hung between them, seemingly resigned to his fate.

"What are you doing, Uncle?"

"Samson is being brought to trial," he said. A wicked grin spread across his face. "There will be blood tonight."

CHAPTER 12

Delilah had never been to a trial for an execution before. She sat in the box next to her father along with the senators and their families, as befitting her station. Usually, this was a place where her father took her to listen to the dreary proceedings relating to disagreements between disgruntled merchants. All around the top of the building, Delilah saw that people were hanging out over the balconies. The noise reminded her of the time that she had accidentally stepped into a bee hive in a fallen tree. The theatre buzzed with activity. Tension filled the air like tiny needles. The bodies swarmed; talk sounded like an angry drone. The air felt thick as honey, it was warm and smelled rank. Now, Delilah worried for Samson. Would she be able to save him from the wrath of the people?

Delilah watched as Achaziah led the procession. She saw Samson enter the theatre, then. His hands were tied before him; his jailers pulled him along like an ox toward the columns in the centre of the theatre.

Samson looked no better than he had in the jail. Worse, Delilah thought, now that she could see every scar outlined in the late afternoon sun as it drifted down through the windows and to the central stage. His face looked sunken and skull-like. Near death. But she could no more look away from him than she could turn away from a child born dead. No, her heart was tangled like uncombed hair. She watched as Samson was tied to the pillars and forced to face the Senators. A roar travelled around the theatre; it beat upon Delilah's heart. Achaziah raised his arms and waited for silence to address the crowd.

"This man is charged with murder. He is charged with breaking a treaty. And he is charged with oath-breaking." He turned to face Samson. "Do you deny these charges?"

Samson stood dumbly before the crowd.

"I ask you again: do you deny these charges?"

Silence was his only answer.

The crowd whispered.

"Will you give no answer? If you do not answer, you will die."

Samson said nothing. Delilah jumped up then, and ran toward Achaziah. "I deny the charges."

"You are not his counsel, sit down, Delilah."

"I will not," Delilah answered.

"Then you too will answer for him, and if he is found guilty, you too will suffer."

Delilah nodded her understanding.

"To the first charge of murder, I charge Samson with murder."

"If you mean your sons, Achaziah, you, as head of this army, should know that those who kill or are killed while engaged in combat are not considered murders. Your sons were strong and capable fighters. If Samson cut them down, then he did so honorably. I deny your charge and ask it to be removed from your complaints."

The Senators conferred for a moment. Soon a response rose from among them. "We agree to drop this from our complaints." A murmur ran through the crowd.

"The second charge was that of breaking a treaty. I charge that Samson is guilty of breaking his oath to our people to cease hostilities. News has come to us that the Israelites are preparing to attack again."

"It is true," Delilah answered, "the Israelites are preparing to attack once more." Grumbling rose from the crowd. "However, Samson himself refused to fight." She walked close to him and showed the crowd his hands. The places where Samson's thumbs should have been were black. "These," she said, "are the hands of a man who refused to take arms against us because of his promise. And these are the hands that his own people mutilated for failing to support their plans."

"Is it true?" Whispers ran through the theatre.

Achaziah nodded. "Yes, the prisoner was found to already be without thumbs when we captured him."

"Then he cannot be charged with breaking the treaty." The Senate proclaimed.

"I did not say breaking the treaty," Achaziah said. "I said that he broke his oaths, his oaths to you." He pointed to Delilah.

"That is hardly a crime worth punishing here," Delilah refuted. "Samson is my husband and what wrongs we have done each other are for us to correct and for our gods to mete out justice. We have made our peace with each other. It is not for you to try and deem wrong or right."

"So you do not deny that he has wronged you?"

"I do not deny it. But I have also wronged him."

"You are not on trial, Delilah. Do you deny that he confined you to a tent?"

"I do not; yet it was only for my safety during the time that our home was being built."

"Do you deny that he struck you?"

"I do not. But he was ill and could not control his actions."

"He struck you more than once."

"Yes, he did. But the last time he did so, it was because I stepped in front of my slave who would not follow the rules of his house. It was an accident." Voices rumbled around the theatre. "He did not mean to harm me," she said loudly. Delilah thought back to the night of Samson's capture. How he had returned and made amends for his wrongdoing. "And he made compensation for his error," Delilah whispered.

She realized then, just how badly she had wronged Samson. She had left him without consolation and comfort. Had not been a support to him through his incarceration. She had not dared to stand for him, no, she had abandoned him. The trial did not seem to be going well now. What could she do to make amends? How could she show Samson her love, and her desire to make right all the wrongs between them?

Delilah saw the handle of a dagger and seized it from the soldier who stood beside Samson. He moved to take it from her but she moved quickly away. She wrapped her hair around one hand and raised the blade to the side of her throat. "Stand back," she shouted, "else two will die today."

"Delilah, no!" her father mouthed. Delilah deafened herself to his pleas. She pulled her hair down and thrust the blade upward. She held a fistful of hair in one hand, the blade in the other. She moved rapidly toward Samson, and dropped the hair at his feet.

"I have wronged you, Samson. I have not been a wife to you. I ask that you accept my penance for all I have done that has harmed you. Take my strength and live," Delilah offered.

"My strength comes from YHVH," Samson affirmed." My life is not mine, it has always belonged to YHVH." Delilah shook her head in disbelief.

"No, Samson, do not die."

"I do not die today; I go to live with my father." Delilah clung to him. "No Delilah, I am ready to meet my father in Heaven. Your people would only destroy you if you stay. Your death would deny our life together. Go, so long as you live, my love goes with you."

"And mine with you," Delilah answered. She heard Samson begin to sing to his god. It was the same song she had heard the night that she had cut his hair. The same song that he had sung the night that her uncle had taken him. Her heart rose into her throat then fell into her feet. Delilah's hands dropped to her sides. The dagger dropped to the ground. She felt numb to the firm hands of her father's servants as they grabbed her by the wrists and dragged her out of the theatre. Standing by the entrance, she could see how the crowd was becoming agitated. They had come for a trial and a stoning. They would not be denied. It was chaos. Rocks rained through the chamber. Some hit Samson, bruising him, cutting him. Chants of Samson rose and fell. Murderer! Oath breaker! Invectives were hurled at him like stones. Delilah imagined every hurt against him as if it was to her.

Her body ached with every stone that slammed against Samson. He was unable to free himself from the onslaught. Delilah stood in the courtyard; her feet seemed to grow roots to hold her and make her bear witness to his suffering. She could not walk away from him; she felt bound to Samson beyond this time and place.

Through the din, Delilah did not notice the ground trembling. Rocks fell from the top of the theatre, but she thought that the violence in the theatre was its source. Something fell and broke nearby. Reddish clay powder clouded the air; part of a statue rolled to Delilah's feet. She stooped to pick it up. It was El's head. Delilah looked up. She saw the crest of the temple begin to sway. "The Temple of El! It is crumbling!" she shouted.

Over the clamor in the theatre, no one heard her. She watched as people, poor and rich, young and old, stepped out of the buildings and looked at the sky. Buildings all around her were shaking, pieces broke off and fell, crashing to the ground. Delilah's feet would not move from where she stood. People scrambled to get away from the falling buildings. The frenzy to kill Samson had become a desperate need to leave a building that was starting to collapse. The only sounds she heard now were grunts as people pushed each other aside to the nearest doors and swarmed to escape. Others poured out the windows and fell to the ground below. A growing pile of bodies lay there.

As the sun dipped lower on the horizon, Delilah could just make out Samson's shape. He was still hanging between the two central columns, his head hung low, and his arms outstretched and his legs splayed wide apart and bound so he could not move. Achaziah stood beside him. He yelled at people not to fear and that El, the Almighty God of Justice would punish those who were unfaithful.

In the crush of people leaving the theatre, Delilah saw Samson. He raised his head and looked into the blazing sun.

"Into your hands, Father, I commend my spirit," he shouted over the noise. His arms strained against the chains, which groaned as they tightened. Delilah watched as Samson collapsed into a heap between the columns. There was a grinding noise… a rumbling… and then a terrible jumbling of rocks like demons throwing bones.

She watched as the columns fell first and smothered the Senator's box. Without its supports, the theatre crumbled inwardly into a pile of rocks. People outside the theatre cried out to those inside the theatre. Shouts erupted on both sides of the rock. All around her, people were rushing to find loved ones, alive or dead. She didn't know how long she stood there before she thought to move and find her own. Her thoughts stopped her before she stirred.

Her husband was most likely dead. And if not dead, he would not want to be kept alive, a shadow of who he had once been. Her Uncle deserved to die for the cruelty he had inflicted on Samson. Her father, she knew, had been in the front row of the Senator's box, unable to escape his fate. She was certain he was dead. She hugged herself and began to wail for her dead. Her voice was but one voice in the chorus that rose around the theatre.

She walked instinctively back to her father's home and to her chamber, away from the theatre, away from sorrow, away from death. The servants were silent, out of respect or fear, Delilah did not know. They, at least, helped each other. How unlike her own people, who used people, thinking themselves to be gods. She hated her people. She hated how she had been used. How Samson had been used.

A withered woman entered the chamber and watched as Delilah appraised her possessions. What good would a golden diadem of El do for her? Delilah thought. Surely it had value, but only for a priestess. And she was dead too.

"Here," Delilah said, "take this."

The woman gasped. "I cannot! I will be called a thief!"

Delilah took a scroll from a table near her bed and wrote a short message. "Now you will not be accused of stealing from your master. Keep this with you, and take your family wherever you choose. You are free."

Delilah fingered the signet ring that her mother had worn. She slipped it on her finger. This was her heirloom. The rest she took was to be sold, except for a change of clothes and a few tools. She packed a pouch and stole out of the house like a thief. The servant returned and tried to accompany her.

"No," Delilah said, "where I must go, I must go alone."

"But it is dangerous for a woman to travel alone."

Delilah nodded: "But I will not be alone. I am meeting a caravan by the desert well," she lied.

"May El be merciful, may the Great Bull be gentle, may the Serpent Queen give comfort, may the River of life sustain you," the servant said.

"And you," Delilah returned the familiar parting phrase of every caravan that left to enter the desert. Delilah turned away from the city and began to climb toward the mountains. Every step took her further away from her people, her husband and her past.

CHAPTER 13

Delilah tucked her parcel closer to her, pressing it into her back. It carried her necessities. A few jewels, a water skin, a change of clothes, a coal to start a fire with and a bucket to carry it in. She carried her memories; and something else. Self knowledge made her realize what she had been trying to deny for more than a moon. Her cycle had not come since the night that she and Samson had lain together.

She climbed up the mountain, following the path that the caravans had made through season after season of trade across the desert. The sound of wailing rose from the ancient city and reached Delilah above. The keening matched the achy feeling in her chest. Delilah hugged herself and rubbed her belly half in wonder and half in fear. The fire would keep fierce animals away, but it was the spirits of her dead that haunted her. She could only go forward if she exorcised herself of them.

Delilah breathed in the sweet smell of burning cedar. Delilah felt broken like the theatre. All her supports were gone. Her mother long dead. Her best friend. Her father. Her husband. Her uncle. Her people. Samson's people. Every column crumbled and broken. She let the cleansing scent wash over her as she hummed a prayer to El.

Delilah sang a lament for the man she loved. She danced on tired feet for her broken family. When the ghosts came and danced with her, Delilah said her goodbyes to her mother and her father, her cousins and her uncle. She danced, then, one last time with Samson. He clung to her, and she to him and to the life they could have had. But Delilah knew that she could not stay with him, and he could not stay in her world. She turned away, tears filling her eyes and clapped a rhythm of hope and life for herself and for her unborn child. She clapped and danced and sang until weariness made her rest. She pulled a blanket around her and fell asleep.

She dreamed of the desert again. The fields of sand and an oasis. Cool water. Life. She reached out to hold it in her hands.

The promise of sunlight peeking over the mountainside woke Delilah. She stared at the burnt out fire. The darkness was cold and windy. If she hoped to make it to the well before nightfall, Delilah needed to go now.

Her dreams of the desert made sense now. There, like in her dreams, her footsteps would be erased and perhaps, she hoped, the pain of the past would drift away like the blowing sand. There was water and renewal on the other side of the desert.

Steadily, Delilah followed the caravan path up the mountain. At the top, she gasped. The sun blazed above her. The desert lay below her. It shimmered in blinding beauty. It's enormous, she thought.

The path zigzagged along the mountainside, making its way closer and closer to the desert. Delilah followed it to the end and went to go to the well. Its white stones stood out like bare bones on the earth. She made a place to rest and slept at the base of the mountain. The wind from the desert whipped up sand. It put her fire out. She rose to the sun glaring at her through the branches of the scrub trees at the base of the mountain. A figure stood in front of her. His robes were as dirty as before. His hair was wild, matted and greasy. His hands were caked in soil. He grinned as he approached Delilah and looked into her eyes.

"Where are you going?" the prophet asked.

"I do not know."

"Is God with you?"

"Yes."

"Then go with God."

Delilah stepped toward the desert. She lifted her veil to shield her eyes from the wind-whipped sand. The heat pressed in against her, trying to suck the life out of her. But she was an oasis in the desert. She carried life within her. Her heart leapt with joy while her feet carried her away from the mountains and her people.

From time to time, Delilah turned her head to look back from whence she came. She saw that her footprints were already vanishing in the changing desert. Her best friend and servant had deserted her. Her family was dead. Her husband was dead. Her people were gone. She had no home; but she belonged. She raised her voice in praise, thanking her god of many names, knowing that her prayers were heard and answered.

###

ABOUT THE AUTHOR

Maude Stephany is fascinated with Story and how it brings people together. She is a member of CANSCAIP and her work has been published in international children's and parenting magazines. In addition to writing her own stories, Maude uses her skills as a writer and a speaker to help others to tell their stories and works as an editor and professional ghostwriter.

Author: Maude Stephany - Edited by Yvan C. Goudard

Published by Rhetorical Ratatouille

Learn more about Rhetorical Ratatouille on

http://www.rhetorical-ratatouille.com

14398273R00068

Made in the USA
Charleston, SC
09 September 2012